For my wife Jenée, and all the kids who honor me ....
Jenée, you inspire, and your experience inspired this book. Thank you.

"Daddy Why Am I Brown?"

A healthy conversation about skin color and family.

By, Bedford Palmer II, Ph.D.

Visit my website for more information: www.drbfpalmer.com
Like me on Facebook www.facebook.com/drbfpalmer

This is Joy... Joy is a little girl with terra-cotta brown skin with a warm golden undertone.

Joy looks at her Mommy and looks at her Daddy, and she notices that they are not the same color as she is.

Joy's Mommy has fawn beige colored skin that has a warm golden undertone.

Joy's Daddy has russet brown skin
that has a warm copper undertone.

One day Joy asks her Daddy, "Daddy, why does Mommy's skin, and your skin, and my skin, all have different colors?"

Her Daddy closes his computer, picks Joy up, and sits her in his lap.

Joy's Daddy takes a breath and says,
"Well, Babygirl, that is a very good question
and I will tell you all about it."

First, the reason that you have such beautiful brown skin, is that you are the child of your Mommy and me.

That means that you are part me and part Mommy.

Joy makes a face and says,
"I know that, but why are you and Mommy
different colors?"

Joy asks, "Does that mean that if I move to Pópo's house that my skin will look like hers?"

Joy's Daddy chuckles and says, "No Babygirl, not exactly."
He reopens his computer and says,
"Let me show you what I mean."

Joy's Daddy types some things
into the computer and a map of the earth is
on the screen. He says,
"Joy, this is our world, planet Earth."

Here is where we are. And here is where your
Pòpo's family is from in Asia.
The people who are from that area of the world
usually look like your Pòpo.

Joy asks, "Why doesn't Mommy look just like Pópo?"

Joy's Daddy explains, "That is because your mommy's dad comes from a family that started off living here, like my Mommy and Daddy."

Africa

Joy's Daddy tells her,
"Well, all the people, everywhere, have a story.
And all those stories are different.
So, people look different in lots of different ways."

Joy's Daddy goes on to say,
"If you have light skin, it usually means that your
ancestors come from a place where it is colder and less sunny.
And if you have darker skin, it usually means that your ancestors
come from a place that is warmer and sunnier."

Joy asks, "But why did living near the middle make our ancestors darker?"

"See, Babygirl, people who have dark skin are better protected from the sun" says Joy's Daddy.
"And people who have lighter skin and lived in places that have less sunlight did not need the extra protection where they were."

Joy's Daddy looks at her thoughtfully and smiles, and says, "Do you want to know a secret?"

Joy nods her head, and says, "Yes!"

Joy's Daddy tells her, "A lot of people think that they can judge a person based on their skin."

Joy's Daddy answers, "Yes, just like that Babygirl."
Then he goes on to say, "But they are wrong."

"Babygirl, the color of their skin does not tell you about their family,
the food that they eat, or the way they talk.
Skin color definitely does
not tell you if they are good or bad people."

Joy asks, "So how do you know what kind of person they are?"

Joy's Daddy answers, "You can't tell by looking. You have to spend time getting to know them. You have to learn about their family, and their ancestors, and what they like, and what they don't like, and who they see themselves as. Babygirl, you have to take the time to get to know them…"

Joy squishes her face and says, "Daddy, that sounds like a lot of work."

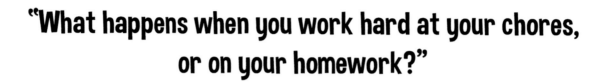

"What happens when you work hard at your chores, or on your homework?"

Joy says, "You get better at it, and you get the right answers..."

Joy's Daddy winks at her and says,
"You are right Babygirl! You do..."

What's Your Skin Color?

Ivory

Porcelan

Pale Ivory

Warm Ivory

Sand Rose

Limestone

Senna

Saddle

Band

Terra Cotta

Bronze

Amber

Sepia

Tawny

Umber

Pearl

Warm Tan

Golden

Deep Bronze

Hickory

Beige

Russet

Gold

Ebony

Vocabulary

Ancestors: a person who was in someone's family in past times : one of the people from whom a person is descended.

Continent: one of the great divisions of land (such as North America, South America, Europe, Asia, Africa, Australia, or Antarctica) of the Earth.

Country: an area of land that is controlled by its own government.

Culture: the beliefs, customs, arts, etc., of a particular society, group, place, or time.

Equator: an imaginary circle around the middle of the Earth that is the same distance from the North Pole and the South Pole.

Ethnicity: races or large groups of people who have the same customs, religion, origin, etc.

Discrimination: unfairly treating a person or group of people differently from other people or groups of people.

Heritage: the traditions, achievements, beliefs, etc., that are part of the history of a group or nation.

Melanin: a dark brown or black substance that is a natural part of people's skin, hair, and eyes.

Race: one of the groups that people can be divided into based on certain physical qualities (such as skin color)

Racism: poor treatment of or violence against people because of their race; the belief that some races of people are better than others

Definitions adapted from http://www.learnersdictionary.com

Discussion

1. What is your **favorite** color? Why is it your favorite?

2. What is the most **beautiful** thing about your skin color? What else has the same color like **your skin**?

3. Where does your **family** come from? Who are your **ancestors**?

4. Do the members of your family have **different** skin colors? **Describe** what is beautiful about their different skin.

Activities

1. Look at some of the pictures of your family. Is there a **country** or a region that your family is from? **Go online** together and look for pictures of people from that country or region. Learn three things about the cultures there. **Talk** about the cultural traditions that you still do in your family.

2. Use skin color **crayons** to color in your favorite coloring book. See how **close** you can get to your own skin color.

3. Use the **discussion questions** above to make a **video** to share with your family and friends. Tag us on **Instagram** @deeperthancolor and #DaddyWhyAmIBrown so that we can like and maybe repost your video.

Dr. Bedford Palmer is a licensed psychologist and an Associate Professor at Saint Mary's College of California. He holds a Ph.D. in Counseling Psychology and researches issues related to social justice and cultural factors. Dr. Palmer maintains a small private practice in Oakland California, where he works with a diverse clientele and provides multicultural competence training to individuals and organizations.

He has ten nieces and nephews and a great many little cousins.

Bedford is a self-described huge nerd, who loves sci-fi, anime, and fantasy.

He is happily married to the most amazing woman that he has ever met,

and he has a dog that is definitely smarter and cuter than yours (at least in his eyes).

You can learn more about Dr. Palmer's work at www.drbfpalmer.com,

and you can follow him @drbfpalmer on Twitter and Instagram.